197527

# When I Was Little Like You

VIKING

Published by the Penguin Group
Penguin Books Ltd, 27 Wrights Lane, London W8 5TZ, England
Penguin Books USA Inc., 375 Hudson Street, New York, New York 10014, USA
Penguin Books Australia Ltd, Ringwood, Victoria, Australia
Penguin Books Canada Ltd, 10 Alcorn Avenue, Toronto, Ontario, Canada M4V 3B2
Penguin Books (NZ) Ltd, 182–190 Wairau Road, Auckland 10, New Zealand

Penguin Books Ltd, Registered Offices: Harmondsworth, Middlesex, England

First published 1997
1 3 5 7 9 10 8 6 4 2

Text copyright © Jill Paton Walsh, 1997
Illustrations copyright © Stephen Lambert, 1997

The moral right of the author and illustrator has been asserted

Filmset in Futura Book

Manufactured in China by Imago

A CIP catalogue record for this book is available from the British Library

ISBN 0–670–86799–3

# When I Was Little Like You

Jill Paton Walsh

Illustrated by
Stephen Lambert

VIKING

"Look, Gran," said Rosie.

"Look at the train, Gran."

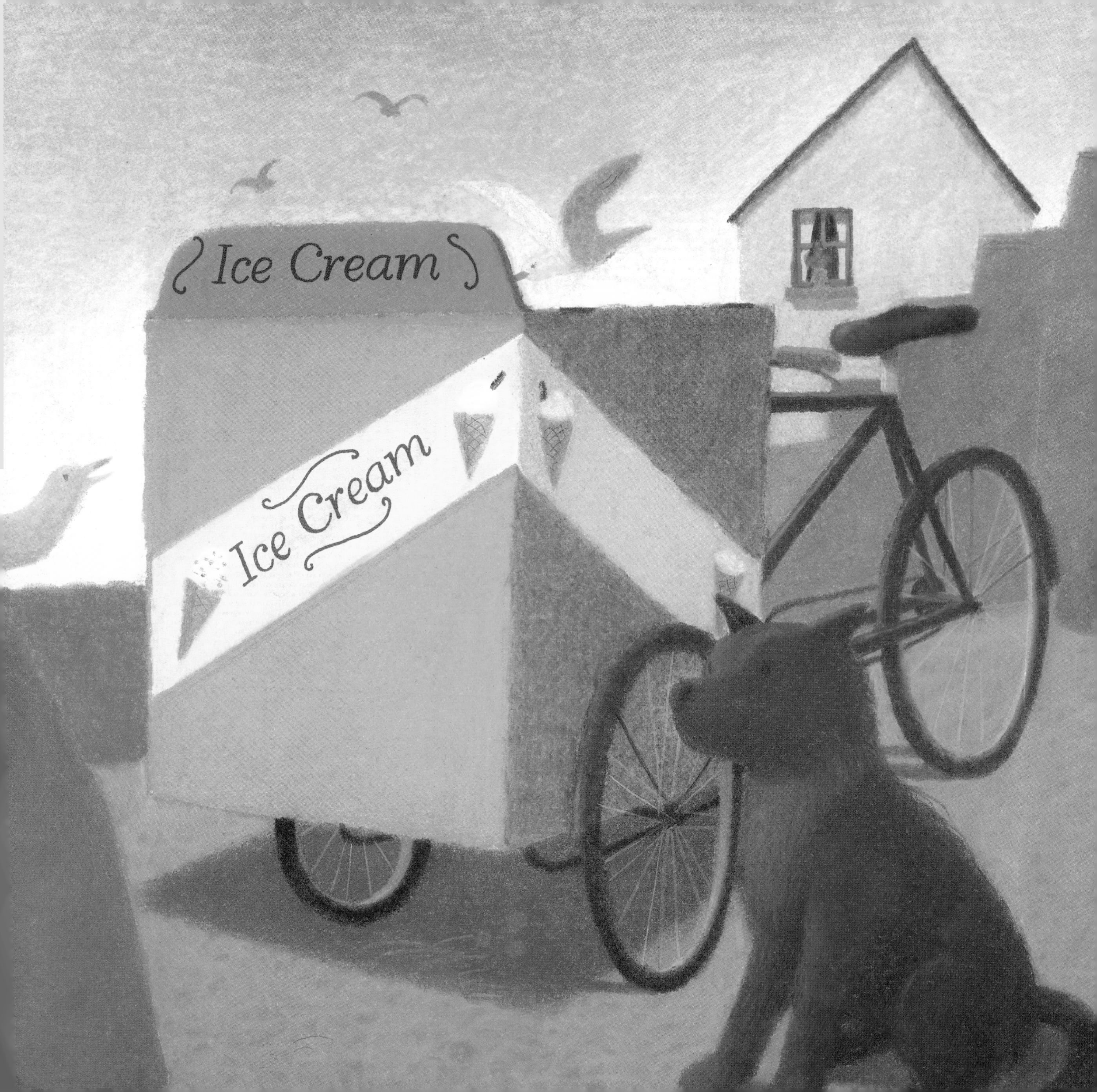
Ice Cream
Ice Cream

"Look, Gran," said Rosie.
"Look at the boats, Gran."

"When I was little like you," said Gran, "the ice-cream seller was a man on a bicycle. He had a sign that said 'Stop me and Buy One'."

"Look, Gran," said Rosie.
"Look at the ice-cream van."

"When I was little like you," said Gran, "a steam engine pulled the carriages. It made little home-made clouds as it puffed round the headland."

"When I was little like you," said Gran, "the boats had brown sails, not engines. They couldn't get out of the harbour unless the wind would let them."

"Look, Gran," said Rosie.
"Look at the fish shop, Gran."

Closed

fresh fish

"When I was little like you," said Gran, "we bought fish from the boatmen on the quay. A brace of bright mackerel for supper, still fresh and shining."

"Look, Gran," said Rosie.
"Look at the sweets, Gran."

"When I was little like you," said Gran, "the sweets were in rows of glass bottles. We bought them at four for a penny, or one for a farthing."

"Look, Gran," said Rosie.
"Look at the surfers, Gran."

"When I was little like you," said
Gran, "nobody knew how to do that.
When the waves were wild we played
catch-as-catch-can with the breakers."

"Look, Gran," said Rosie.
"Look at the lighthouse, Gran."

"When I was little like you," said Gran, "the lighthouse looked just like that on fine summer evenings."

"Did you like the world better, Gran, the way it was when you were little like me?"

"Oh no, my dear, no! The world is more fun by far now it has you in it!"